To Evia
♡ M. Power

A Childs Book Of
Flowers
Through Poetry

By Margaret Power

A Childs Book Of Flowers Through Poetry by Margaret Power

A Childs Book Of Flowers Through Poetry by Margaret Power

Praise the Gardener

The Gardener who grows,

Flowers such as those,

Beauty he bestows,

Our worries and our woes,

Suddenly have froze,

When we see the rose.

Flowers to Bestow

First the grass I mow, Next the ground I hoe,

With some seeds I sow, Then inside I go.

I come to see but no, I bend down real low,

Still nothing here to show, Growing oh so slow.

To pass some time I sew, and, sew, and sew, and sew.

Then I say hello, At last they start to grow.

Very tall they grow, Their beauty inspires me so,

I paint just like Van Gogh, Flowers to bestow.

What Scent?

The scent flows,

Up your nose,

Lie back,

Is it lilac?

This fragrance we'll unlock,

Perhaps night scented stock?

Maybe jasmine,

Has won?

I know its honeysuckle,

So sweet it makes you chuckle.

Decorations

How to make a garden pretty?

I will tell you with this ditty,

Poppy seeds, although itty, bitty,

Can brighten up this city.

For my first tip,

To convert a kip,

It's easy to flip,

Just plant the tulip.

Another place to focus,

Carpeted below us,

Plant a purple crocus,

Its beauty you will notice.

Flowers for Romance

Strolling in a sea of blue,

Hyacinth made it true.

Growing on a tee-pee,

The lightly scented sweet pea.

Over near the river,

He has a rose to give her.

Lilies bright and white,

Dancing in the moonlight.

Given in advance,

Flowers for romance.

Favorite

The Hollyhock stands tall,

Up against my garden wall

Beside it is the Tutsan,

Like a huge yellow fan,

Fluffed out like a feather,

Here is some purple Heather.

Watch in the grass,

A Cowslip you might pass,

Like a skirt, all frilly,

I have a garden Lily,

Purple is my Mallow,

It grows all long and narrow.

But Jasmine smells the prettiest,

It is the one that I love best,

16

What about you?

Do you have a favorite too?

Sunflower

Tall like a watch tower,

Turns to charge with solar power,

Loves every rain shower,

The beautiful, golden Sunflower.

Flos Solis maior.

In the Garden

Roses creeping,

Wisteria weeping,

Lilac sleeping,

Daffodil peeping,

Violets leaping,

Marigolds keeping,

Gardener sweeping.

Power

Theres a lot of kinds of power,

We have got electric power,

Or the hot bright solar power,

I cannot leave out Hydro power,

We've even caught the wind power,

I've not forgot nuclear power,

But the last spot, to really empower,

Fill up your pot with Flower Power.

Lilac

"I do beg your pardon,

What's that growing in your garden?

The smell is so divine,"

"To ask that is just fine,

Lilac is the name,

I love it just the same.

LILAC

Lavender

Once a weary traveler,

Found himself sat under,

A bunch of lovely lavender,

He smelled and examined her,

For his love he gathered her,

And now for sure has married her.

LAVENDER.

Snowdrop

With your boot,

Watch out for this shoot,

Look and stop,

It's a tiny snowdrop,

Such a delicate beaute.

Daffodil

As the snow goes,

Do you know what grows?

The daffodil,

It will,

Grow in yellow rows.

Wild Flowers

Grab a cup of coffee, Sit outside and look,

Soon you will see, Flowers we often overlook,

Like the soft red poppy.

Sometimes there is clover, Four leafed maybe,

Another wild grower, Is the little daisy,

You never know what might pop up,

Gods already designed it,

The dandelion, buttercup,

and violet.

The Fairies Cupboard

In my garden, I uncovered,

A little fairies cupboard,

Inside I found bluebell hats,

And woven grass combats,

A pretty petal dress,

Clearly made to impress,

But the best thing of all,

Was a rose gown for a ball.

Printed in Great Britain
by Amazon

46879802R00023